# Dream Away

For our westside crew: Kyle, Jack, Joey, Ryan, Bridget & Will
–J. D. & K. B. T.

For David, Grace, and Brownie
–R. G.

ACKNOWLEDGMENTS

I would like to thank Julia Maguire and Chloë Foglia, who were always right,
and especially Kevin Lewis, who took a house tour.–R. G.

SIMON & SCHUSTER BOOKS FOR YOUNG READERS
An imprint of Simon & Schuster Children's Publishing Division
1230 Avenue of the Americas, New York, New York 10020
Text copyright © 2011 by Julia Durango and Katie Belle Trupiano • Illustrations copyright © 2011 by Robert Goldstrom
All rights reserved, including the right of reproduction in whole or in part in any form.
SIMON & SCHUSTER BOOKS FOR YOUNG READERS is a trademark of Simon & Schuster, Inc.
For information about special discounts for bulk purchases, please contact
Simon & Schuster Special Sales at 1-866-506-1949 or business@simonandschuster.com.
The Simon & Schuster Speakers Bureau can bring authors to your live event.
For more information or to book an event, contact the Simon & Schuster Speakers Bureau at
1-866-248-3049 or visit our website at www.simonspeakers.com.
Book design by Chloë Foglia • The text for this book is set in Nicolas Cochin.
The illustrations for this book are rendered in oil on cotton.
Manufactured in China • 0411 SCP
2 4 6 8 10 9 7 5 3 1
Library of Congress Cataloging-in-Publication Data
Durango, Julia, 1967–
Dream away / Julia Durango and Katie Belle Trupiano ; illustrated by Robert Goldstrom.—1st ed.
p. cm.
Summary: At bedtime, a young boy looks forward to falling asleep and
dreaming about sailing the ocean of stars with his father.
ISBN 978-1-4169-8702-4 (hardcover)
[1. Stories in rhyme. 2. Bedtime–Fiction. 3. Dreams–Fiction.
4. Father and child–Fiction.] I. Trupiano, Katie Belle. II. Goldstrom,
Robert, ill. III. Title.
PZ8.3.D933Dp 2011
[E]–dc22
2009042301

# Dream Away

Words by

Julia Durango and Katie Belle Trupiano

Illustrated by

Robert Goldstrom

Simon & Schuster Books for Young Readers

NEW YORK   LONDON   TORONTO   SYDNEY

Dream away, dream away, sleepyhead, love.
Set sail for the ocean of stars up above.
You be the captain and I'll be your mate.
We'll journey together, the heavens await.

In a dream we did float in an old paper boat.

A magic wind blew and delivered our crew.

A rogue band they were: two pixies, one cur,

a winged horse in flight, and a wandering knight.

In a dream the full moon was a yellow balloon.
We followed its trail and grabbed on to its tail.

We played with a bear, an archer, a hare.

A dragon gave chase, but our crew won the race.

Dream away, dream away, sleepyhead, love.

Set sail for the ocean of stars up above.

You be the captain and I'll be your mate.

We'll journey together, the heavens await.

In a dream we did glide down a glimmering slide.
The stars waved good-bye. Mr. Moon winked an eye.

We returned to the seas, and with the next breeze,

our crew took their leave on that magical eve.

In a dream we did float in an old paper boat.
The waves sang a song while the wind hummed along.

They rocked us to sleep on that ocean so deep.
Adrift on the sea—just us—you and me.

Dream away, dream away, sleepyhead, love.

Set sail for the ocean of stars up above.

You be the captain and I'll be your mate.

We'll journey together, the heavens await.